For Jake J A, with love ~ M C B

For Kerry James ~ T M

LITTLE TIGER PRESS
An imprint of Magi Publications
1 The Coda Centre, 189 Munster Road, London SW6 6AW
www.littletigerpress.com

First published in Great Britain 2011
Text copyright © M Christina Butler 2011
Illustrations copyright © Tina Macnaughton 2011
M Christina Butler and Tina Macnaughton have asserted their
rights to be identified as the author and illustrator of this work
under the Copyright, Designs and Patents Act, 1988

A CIP catalogue record for this book is available from the
British Library

All rights reserved • ISBN 978-1-84895-241-6

Printed in China • LTP/1800/0214/0411

10 9 8 7 6 5 4 3 2 1

One Christmas Night

M Christina Butler   *Illustrated by* Tina Macnaughton

LITTLE TIGER PRESS
London

It was nearly Christmas and
Little Hedgehog just could not wait.
"Mince pies and Christmas
cake – yum yum!" he laughed.
"Ooh, now I can put up the big shiny
star that Badger gave me."

"Perfect!" cried Little Hedgehog as he fixed the star to the very top of his tree.

Then he opened Badger's card. "How lovely," he said. It had a huge, glittering Christmas tree on the front.

"Oh dear! My house isn't Christmassy and my tree doesn't sparkle like that," he sighed.

Just then a *rat-a-tat-tat!* came at the door.

"Happy Christmas!" cried Mouse.

"Thank you," said Little Hedgehog.

"But Mouse, I don't know what to do!

My house just isn't Christmassy at all."

"We'll soon fix that," Mouse smiled.

"We can make pine cones sparkle
with glitter," said Mouse as they
tramped into the woods.

"Take cover!" cried Little Hedgehog
as the cones came tumbling down.

"There's holly for the fireplace," Mouse said.
     "Ouch!" squeaked Little Hedgehog. "It has
more prickles than me!"

"Chestnuts and acorns, and big bowls
of berries!" they all sang as they
marched home.

Together they glued and glittered until nuts
and acorns twinkled like stars, and holly twigs
shimmered red, green and gold.

"Wow!" cried Little Hedgehog.
  "It's like a magic Christmassy
cave!" said Mouse. "But we have
to go. We haven't wrapped our
presents yet."

"Oh no!" squeaked Little Hedgehog. "Presents? I've forgotten to get presents for my friends!"

Little Hedgehog thought hard. "I know – I can give this book to Badger!"

"I'll make a carrot cake for Rabbit."

"And a night-time picture for Fox."

"I can make stockings full of nuts for the little ones," chuckled Little Hedgehog, pattering into the wood again.

He gazed up at the glittering branches as snowflakes floated past his nose. "And a big bunch of twinkly twigs for Mouse," he smiled.

Little Hedgehog wandered on and on through the trees, looking for the best twigs he could find. The wood grew darker and the snowflakes swirled faster around him.

"Phew!" he gasped, struggling
with the basket. "However
shall I get home?"

At last the snow stopped, and a bright
moon peeped above the trees. Pale blue
shadows flitted here and there as Little
Hedgehog huffed and puffed through the
snow. Then, in the stillness, he heard a
pad-pad-padding noise getting closer and
closer, until . . .

...CRASH!

"Eeek!" yelped Fox, bumping into Little Hedgehog.

"You look like a walking
Christmas tree!"

Little Hedgehog and Fox
chuckled and chatted all
the way back home.

Fox put the presents round the tree. "Everything looks lovely!" he said.

But Little Hedgehog was not sure. "There is *still* something missing."

Suddenly, a loud knock came at the door . . .

. . .and in walked Badger, with Rabbit and the mice.
"Of course!" squeaked Little Hedgehog, clapping
his paws. "That's what was missing – all of my friends!
Happy Christmas, everyone!"